Stories Through the Rainbow

A collection of short stories

Written by Melissa Gijsbers

Dedication

To Jesse, one of the people who helped me get my confidence back and encouraged me to see the importance of short story collections for readers.

Table of Contents

Dedication..iii

Table of Contents iv

Introduction...1

Red – Why I'm Late for Class 3

Orange – The Toy Was a Squid 7

Yellow – Letter to Myself 10

Green – Escape Room...15

Blue – The Birthday Party 18

Indigo – The Perfect Cup of Tea.................................21

Violet – Neat As A Pin 25

Writing Prompts 28

About the Author...30

Also by Melissa Gijsbers: 32

Introduction

For as long as I can remember, I have loved writing short stories. I also enjoy writing plays, poems, and novels, but short stories have been my favourite thing to write. There are hundreds of short stories floating around in notebooks and on my computer.

I also love working with young writers and inspiring them to be creative and have fun writing.

In 2024, I created a 'Write Through the Rainbow' program for writers, young and old, to write a short story collection with seven stories, each one featuring a colour of the rainbow, and publish it.

Before the first sessions began, I realised I hadn't put together one of my own! With this in mind, I went through short stories that I've written over the years to find stories that have colours in them or can have colours added.

This is that collection.

As you're reading the stories, see if you identify how I've used the designated colours.

Each story came from a writing prompt delivered at a writers' group, and I have included those prompts at the end of the book if you would like to try them yourself, with or without the colours.

I hope you enjoy this collection of short stories.

Happy Reading

Melissa Gijsbers

Red – Why I'm Late for Class

I am usually a punctual person. I pride myself on getting places early as it was drummed into me at a young age that being late was rude and unacceptable. My friends tease me about this as they are usually 'fashionably late', even to school. But it's something that is just not me...

This morning, I left for school as usual. It was my normal time so I could walk to the bus stop, get on the early bus so I would get a seat, and be at school in plenty of time before the first bell. But today was no ordinary trip.

Walking out of my house started like any other day. Until I spotted a kid riding a small unicorn! I couldn't believe my eyes.

Then, a tiny, red helicopter flew past, narrowly missing my ear, followed by a leprechaun with a remote control in his hands, banging into me, causing the strap on my school bag to break and the contents to spill out onto the road.

The road wasn't its usual self either. For some reason, it was now made of chocolate, and my books were splattered with it. By the time I got to the bus stop, I had missed my usual bus, or so I thought.

A few minutes later, instead of a bus, a tugboat pulled up, floating on the river of chocolate that was the road. It was weird, but I got on anyway, worried I would be late.

The tugboat didn't follow the usual route to school, instead, it went only where the chocolate river went, taking twice as long the bus did to arrive.

At the closest stop to school, I was greeted by a fire-breathing dragon who had set up residence in the front yard of one of the houses in the street. I had to wait for it to have a nap before I could pass.

Then, there were two men having a sword-fighting duel near the school gates. The other strap of my school bag was sliced through, sending my books flying once again.

By the time I had picked them up, the bell had gone, and I hadn't reached my locker yet!

I tried running through the grounds, only to have an army of lollipops block my path. Thankfully, they were small and their jelly weapons ineffectual, so I jumped over them and made my way to the locker bay.

I was so late, the locker bay was already locked for class time. So, I made my way to class, dodging a hailstorm of angry paintbrushes on the way.

Finally, I took my seat at the back of the classroom. You may not believe me, but I swear it's true. This is why I'm late to class today.

Orange – The Toy Was a Squid

Christie said the toy was a squid. Christie said a lot of things. They didn't always make sense.

The toy in question was clearly a teddy bear. It had bright blue fur that sparkled in the sunlight. A pale green bow was tied around its neck and it had sparkly eyes.

In no way did it resemble a squid, even if Christie said it did.

I should have known better than to argue.

'The toy is a teddy bear,' I told Christie with what I hoped was a matter-of-fact tone.

'It's a squid,' Christie said, so sure of herself with a 'take no nonsense' vibe about her. 'It's clearly a squid. And that one is a goat.' She pointed to a toy car.

Usually, I would play her games, but today was not a usual day. I was tired of Christie not making sense.

'Grow up,' I said. 'That's a car, not a goat. That's Lego, a doll, mechano.' I pointed to each object. 'That's a squid.' I pointed to a soft toy that was clearly a squid, although I don't know any kid who would want a giant stuffed orange cephalopod. 'The toys are what they are.'

'Grow down,' Christie said. 'It's much more fun to pretend.'

Christie skipped off saying toys were things they clearly weren't. I watched her go. Part of me was jealous of my little sister. I was the one who was always being told to grow up...

in that moment, I decided to take Christie's advice to 'grow down'.

I got Christie's attention and, with a straight face, pointed to a pile of wooden blocks.

'That is a wiggly worm,' I said. She agreed.

Yellow – Letter to Myself

To myself from five years ago,

This is a stupid assignment I have to write for English. We have to write what we'd tell our past self from five years ago. Why five years? It's got something to do with starting high school and, honestly, this seems pretty pointless.

Anyway, to my past self, you'll be happy to know that you've achieved hero status! You may not think this is possible as you enter high school, but you'll get there.

How you ask? Well, it wasn't easy.

For the most part, high school will suck, it will be awful, it will be torture, and you'll want to run away screaming. You'll even try running away from home at one point (just note that tying a yellow pillowcase on the end of a broomstick is a particularly silly thing to do), however, you will achieve hero status in five years' time.

It all started one lunch time when Roland brought a bag of lolly snakes to school. You won't know Roland yet; he came to the school in year nine. To pass the time, we had competitions with the snakes, things like who could pull them the longest before they snapped or who could tie the most knots in them. That sort of thing.

The next day he brought in another bag, and this continued for a week, until, the following Monday, he brought in two bags and we had a competition to see who could eat the bag the fastest. I won that one by more than a snake!

In our little group, I was a legend. Who knew that eating a bag of snakes really fast would be something that others would think is cool?

Anyway, word got around the school and then further afield… to *Maple Leaf High School*, our arch-enemy.

Maple Leaf High School beats us at every sports day, arts festival, music competition, and anything else that we do. I have no idea how the word got to *Maple Leaf*, but it did.

At the annual regional sports day, all the local schools were there, and we were sure *Maple Leaf* were going to win again, and they were up there, however there was a wider spread of results, so much so that by the end of the day, we were tied with them on points! No one could believe it.

It was at that moment that Amanda Benson, one of the *Maple Leaf* school captains, stood up.

'I declare one more event,' she said. No one had seen that coming. We had played all the sports, there was nothing left. 'A snake eating competition!'

I was pushed up to the front, along with Bruiser Jones, a big kid from *Maple Leaf*. They had come prepared with bags of lolly snakes.

Roland gave me a thumbs up as I sat down at the table beside Bruiser, the bags of snakes in front of us.

The rules were simple; we had to consume as many bags of snakes as we could in one minute. This included opening the sealed bags.

Timers were set and we started.

Bruiser made a good start, but I wasn't far behind. It was around the thirty-second mark that I caught up, then surpassed him as his fingers got caught up opening a bag.

Just as the buzzer sounded, I finished the tenth snake out of my third packet. I glanced over at Bruiser. Two empty packets lay in front of him and he was struggling to open his third packet.

I was victorious! I brought home the win for our school. I was a hero!

So, my message to you is that school is going to be hard, but the day will come where you will be the hero, you will be a winner.

Oh, and you probably won't want to eat lolly snakes for a little while too.

From me

Green – Escape Room

The room was dark and empty except for an old mattress in one corner. It had been this way for a while, although Eliza had no idea how long it had been. There was no window in the room, and it took her exactly five steps to get from one side to the other. With nothing else to do, she curled up on the mattress. This wasn't fun.

Out of nowhere, a small, green butterfly landed on her hand.

'Hello little butterfly,' Eliza said quietly. She didn't want to scare it away. 'How did you get in here?'

Eliza had checked out the room when she was first locked in here, but couldn't find a way out. Where had the butterfly come from?

The butterfly flew up around her head, circling three times before landing on an uneven spot on the wall. Eliza reached up to touch the knot in the wood and felt it move under her fingers.

'That's strange,' Eliza said, 'It didn't do that before.'

Without its resting place, the butterfly flew and landed on one of the buttons on the mattress. Eliza followed and tried to push the button. Nothing happened. She looked closer and saw a very small arrow indicating she should twist the button, which she did. The movement startled the butterfly, who flew away.

Eliza watched the butterfly as it went to the door of the room and vanished. Eliza went over to the door and felt around. There was a tiny nail sticking out. She pulled it out, and the door swung open. Before she knew it, she was enveloped in a huge hug.

'About time, Eliza,' her friend, Tarquin, said. 'We thought you were going to stay in there forever!'

'At least until the centre closed...' added Gemma.

'We're never taking you to an escape room again!' Tina said.

'Good,' Eliza said. 'That was all a bit weird.'

Blue – The Birthday Party

Everything was ready. This was going to be the coolest birthday party ever. Her mum sat the birthday cake in the middle of the table. A perfect artist's palette, made entirely of cake and icing.

'What are you wearing?' Jodie exclaimed as she looked up and down at her dad. He had no shirt on and was shuffling about in her sister's mermaid costume, complete with a shiny, blue tail.

'I'm a merman,' he said.

'Put a t-shirt on, Dad,' Jodie said.

'I think you look great,' said her mum.

'Yuck,' Jodie said. Her parents were so mushy it was gross. Before she could say anything else, the doorbell rang. Jodie adjusted her headband, eyes and antenna to complete her alien costume, and answered the front door.

'Can you guess what I am?' Eric, Jodie's best friend, asked as he entered the house. He shoved a gift bag covered in flags into her hands. Jodie looked at him. He looked completely normal, although his hair had a bit of a mohawk.

'Give up?' he asked. Jodie nodded. 'I'm chicken… too chicken to dress up!' he started laughing as if this was the funniest thing ever. Jodie just rolled her eyes.

'Eric,' her mum said, 'I need to film this.' She held up her phone while Eric repeated his joke. Jodie still didn't think it was funny. Thankfully, more guests arrived, so I had a reason to move away.

The night went off without a hitch. Dad was super embarrassing in his merman costume but refused to put on a t-shirt. The cake was delicious, and Eric still wasn't funny.

Indigo – The Perfect Cup of Tea

My grandmother always said that there was nothing so bad that it couldn't be solved with a cup of tea. There's just one problem. I'm pretty sure this latest catastrophe can't be fixed with a cup of tea. Also, I don't know how to make tea. Okay, so I have two problems.

Before I could even think about my first problem, I had to learn how to make a cup of tea. I figured it was worth a try. Nothing else was working.

Since I couldn't see my grandmother to ask her advice, I headed to YouTube, only to find dozens of videos.

The first one demanded you have a fancy tea

pot, tea leaves, tea strainers, and other things that I hadn't heard of before and certainly didn't own. I was also sure they wouldn't be found in the supermarket.

The second video featured people in lab coats telling the viewers how we've all been making tea wrong our entire lives. It wasn't really helpful to me as I hadn't ever made a cup of tea. Also, their methods, both the 'right' and 'wrong' ways, looked nothing like I recall seeing when someone made a cup of tea.

There were videos talking about someone called Earl Grey, whoever he was, discussions about tea bags vs loose leaf tea, mugs vs cups, whether to put the milk in first or last. Even videos showing how ceramic mugs were made.

Looking through the videos, I was getting overwhelmed with information, but was none the wiser about how to make a cup of tea, other than it involved boiling water, tea leaves of some description, and some sort of cup or mug. Milk, sugar, and lemon were optional extras.

I abandoned YouTube and did an Internet search. I found some simple instructions and wondered why I hadn't started here.

Boiling water, tea bag, mug – simple.

A trip to the supermarket for supplies, a bit of trial and error – note, make sure the water has actually boiled, and who knew that tea tastes different the more you leave it in the water? – and I had a near perfect cup of tea. It wasn't quite the same as my grandmother's. I think her special ingredient of love was missing, or her old tea pot gave the tea a unique taste. But I finally had my cup of tea.

I curled up on the couch with my brand new, indigo coloured mug and a chocolate chip biscuit and contemplated my life. Making the tea had taken most of the day. In the process, all thoughts of catastrophe had been pushed aside.

As I sipped my tea and thought about things, the catastrophe didn't seem quite so large.

Maybe my grandmother was right. There was nothing so bad that it couldn't be solved with a cup of tea.

Violet – Neat As A Pin

The house was always a mess whenever mum decided to bring out the sewing machine and make clothes for us. We were never sure if we'd get a hand-made book week costume, or one bought from the op shop at the last minute. Same goes for Christmas, birthdays, or any other special occasion. Today, it was making a dress for my end of year formal.

Mum had discovered a stash of fabric in the hall cupboard, including some bright violet taffeta, and that's how it all began. Now the dining room was an explosion of taffeta, lace, sequins, and anything else mum decided she'd use.

We had to be careful with walking through with bare feet as we were walking on literal pins and needles and didn't want them sticking in our feet.

The dress was starting to look like something from the 1980s, and I tried to tell mum that it was no skin off my back if she didn't complete the dress as Aunt Maggie had given a dress to wear, but she was determined.

She called me in to try the dress on.

'There you go,' she said. 'That fits the bill.'

I stared into the mirror. The dress WAS straight out of the 1980s! There were so many frills and bows. I could easily have been on the cover of Vogue or one of those other magazines. I just needed the poofy hair.

'It's… something,' I said, not wanting to hurt her feelings.

She straightened a bow and said, 'Neat as a pin.'

I looked at the dress in the mirror, then at the

pins that had been spilled. It certainly wasn't neat, nor the pins, but they seemed to match, so I agreed with her.

Writing Prompts

As promised, these are the writing prompts that inspired the stories in this collection. Feel free to use them to have fun with your own writing.

- Write the totally true (as in fantastical, made up) reason you are late for class

- First line prompt: The toy was a squid

- Conversation starter: In Five Years… Hero; add in random words: letter, screaming, bindle

- Choose a random object. Use that object to write a story about an escape

- Random Emojis: Alien, Merman, Birthday Cake, Chicken, Artists Palette, Flag, Movie Camera

- Write a story about the perfect cup of tea

- Choose a cliché and write a story inspired by that cliché (I used 'neat as a pin').

About the Author

Melissa Gijsbers is an author and booklover. Stories have always been a big part of her life and she has been writing them for as long as she can remember.

She started working with young writers in 2013 at the Monash Public Library and has been inspiring them to write by providing them with crazy writing prompts ever since! This group helped Melissa discover how important creative writing can be for wellbeing.

She currently lives in Gippsland in Victoria, Australia and spends quite a bit of time coming up with fun writing ideas for stories, as well as writing more books herself.

You can find out more about Melissa and her books on her website—www.melissagijsbers.com

Also by Melissa Gijsbers:

- My Princess Wears a Superhero Cape
- My Mummy is Evil
- Swallow Me, NOW!
- 3... 2... 1... Done!
- Lizzy's Dragon
- Genie in my Drink Bottle & other writing prompts
- Great Lost Sock Mystery & other writing prompts
- Creative Writing for Wellbeing
- Writing Prompts – Random Words